Fanny &
Margarita

Fanny & Margarita

*Five Stories
About
Two Best Friends*

By
KATE SPOHN

Viking

Learning To Fly

Fanny longs to be tiny,
and sparkly,
and able to fly,
like Tinker Bell.

But Fanny is not a magical fairy;
she is a pear,
and her best friend, Margarita, is a banana.
Still, Fanny is determined.
So she and Margarita practice flying.

They start from the top of the hill,
and flap their arms as they run
down to the bottom.

The big girls snicker,
but Fanny and Margarita don't care.
They are learning to fly.

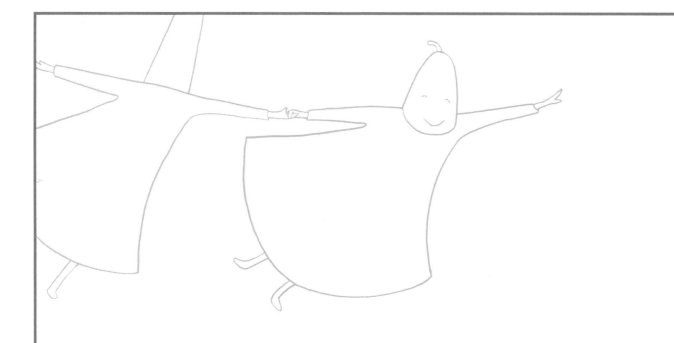

When they run with cardboard wings attached to their
arms, Fanny is sure she feels herself lifting a little.
"This only takes practice," she tells Margarita.
So they keep at it,
knowing someday they will fly.

Feeling Sad

Fanny is sad.

And when she is sad, she eats.

She eats leftover spaghetti,

chocolate chips,

cheese and crackers,

cookies,

pretzels,

ice cream,

peanut-butter crackers,

pound cake,

Doritos,

olives,

and pie.

Margarita comes to see Fanny.

"What are you doing?" she asks.

"I'm feeling sad and miserable,
 and so full I can't move," moans Fanny.

"Well," says Margarita, "maybe if you got out,
 you'd feel better."

"No." Fanny is certain.

"I'm too fat and ugly and sad," she says.
 But Margarita is persuasive.

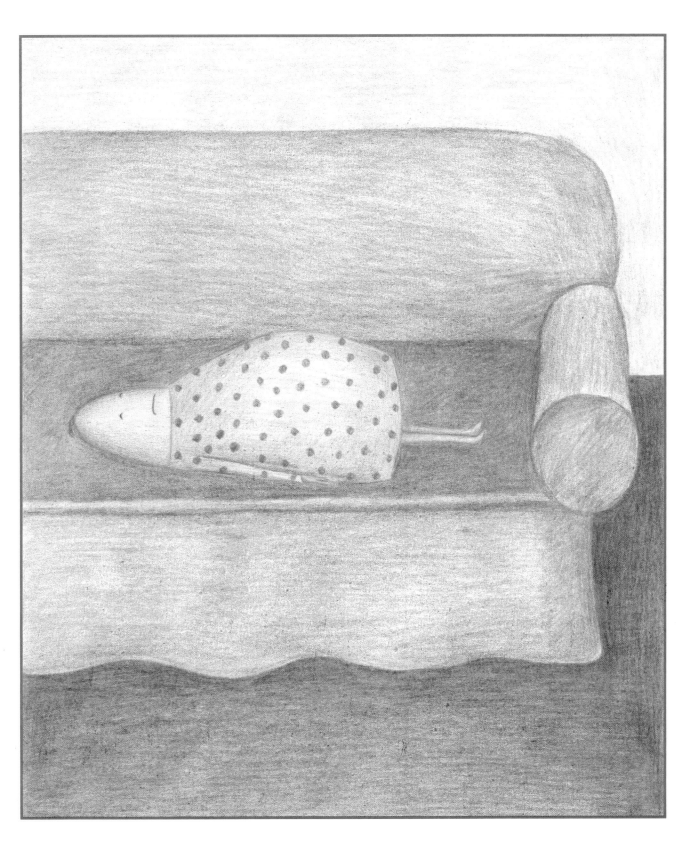

And she is right.

Fanny feels much better once she is out.

"Thanks, Margarita," she tells her best friend.

Between the Raindrops

When it is raining out,
Fanny sits under an umbrella
and watches the rain fall.

Margarita joins Fanny.

"Do you know how to run between the raindrops?" she asks.

"Let's do it!" says Fanny.

So Fanny and Margarita try.

"If the drops were very big, or if we were very small,

we could do it," Fanny tells Margarita.

Then Fanny makes up a song.

She sings, "I like the rain on my umbrella,

I like the rain on my head."

And Margarita finishes:

"I like the rain between the drops.

There it's dry instead!"

Toledo Public Library
173 N.W. 9th St.
Toledo, Oregon 97391

So Fanny and Margarita go inside,
where they can watch the rain,
and be dry too.

A Dancer's Behind

Fanny and Margarita are going to join the dancing club.
They practice in Margarita's room.
Fanny feels like a true dancer until she catches a
glimpse of her behind in the mirror. Then she shrieks.
This, she knows, is no dancer's behind.
"It's the tutu that sticks out," Margarita says, making
Fanny feel better.

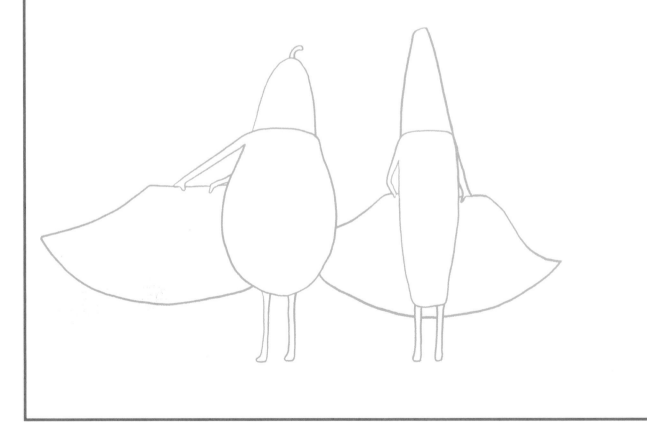

Now, Fanny still isn't sure that she has a dancer's behind, but she is positive she has a true friend.

Fanny's Crush

Fanny is composing a love letter.

Dear Al,
I like you. Do you like me?
Yours,
Fanny

"That is perfect," says Margarita.
And she takes a picture of Fanny.
Then Fanny sends her letter to Al
with her picture enclosed.

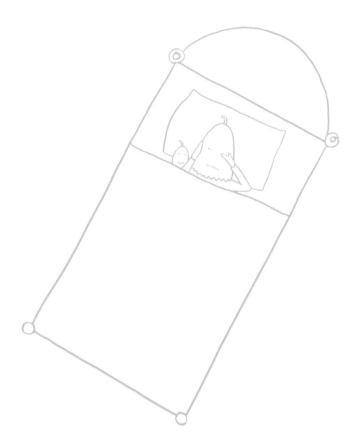

Fanny waits for a response.

She waits two weeks.

But there is no letter from Al.

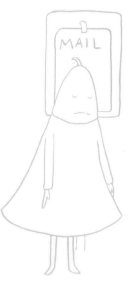

"That's okay, Fanny," Margarita reassures her.
"My brother thinks you're nice.
  And besides, Al isn't very cute,
  or very smart either."

"Margarita, you're my best friend."
"And you're mine," says Margarita.

For Susan Ehlich,
who is as good a friend to me
as Margarita is to Fanny.

VIKING
Published by the Penguin Group
Penguin Books USA Inc., 375 Hudson Street, New York, New York 10014, U.S.A.
Penguin Books Ltd, 27 Wrights Lane, London W8 5TZ, England
Penguin Books Australia Ltd, Ringwood, Victoria, Australia
Penguin Books Canada Ltd, 10 Alcorn Avenue, Toronto, Ontario, Canada M4V 3B2
Penguin Books (N.Z.) Ltd, 182–190 Wairau Road, Auckland 10, New Zealand

Penguin Books Ltd, Registered Offices: Harmondsworth, Middlesex, England

First published in 1993 by Viking, a division of Penguin Books USA Inc.

1   3   5   7   9   10   8   6   4   2

Copyright © Kate Spohn, 1993   All rights reserved

Library of Congress Cataloging-in-Publication Data
Spohn, Kate.
Fanny and Margarita: five stories about two best friends / by
Kate Spohn.   p.   cm.
Summary: Fanny the pear and Margarita the banana share
dreams, adventures, and the joys of a unique friendship.
I S B N 0 - 6 7 0 - 8 4 6 9 2 - 9
[1. Friendship—Fiction.   2. Fruit—Fiction.]   I. Title.
PZ7.S7636Fan   1993   [E]—dc20   92-22208   CIP   AC

Printed in Hong Kong
Set in 20 pt. ITC Goudy Sans Book